Hello, Reader!

The bully takes Max's candy.
The bully says, "I'm going to get you!"

Read the story to find out how Max
saves himself!

For Leslie Margulies,
who isn't big *or* bad.
—T.S.

For Grant and Mara Rose
—P.P.

Text copyright © 1995 by Teddy Slater.
Illustrations copyright © 1995 by Pat Porter.
All rights reserved. Published by Scholastic Inc.
HELLO READER!, CARTWHEEL BOOKS, and the CARTWHEEL BOOKS LOGO
are registered trademarks of Scholastic Inc.

Library of Congress Cataloging-in-Publication Data

Slater, Teddy.
    Who's afraid of the big, bad bully? / by Teddy Slater; illustrated Pat Porter.
        p.   cm. — (Hello Reader! Level 3)
    Summary: Big mean Bertha threatens everyone, especially Max, until he gets a dog.
    ISBN 0-590-90761-1
    [1. Bullies—Fiction.   2. Schools—Fiction.   3. Dogs—Fiction.]
    I. Porter, Pat Grant, ill.   II. Title.   III. Series.
PZ7.S6294Wf   1995
[E]—dc20

94-3323
CIP
AC

12 11 10 9 8 7 6

7 8 9/9 0/0

Printed in the U.S.A.

23

First Scholastic printing, March 1995

Who's Afraid of the
BIG, BAD
BULLY?

by Teddy Slater
Illustrated by Pat Porter

SCHOLASTIC INC.
New York Toronto London Auckland Sydney

CHAPTER ONE:
Who's Afraid of Big Bertha?

Bertha was big. Bertha was mean. Everyone was scared of big, mean Bertha.

All the little girls were scared of Bertha. All the little boys were scared of Bertha.

Even some of the *big* boys were scared of Bertha. She was bigger than they were.

When Bertha said, "Jump!" all the kids jumped.

When Bertha said, "Hand over your candy!" all the kids handed over their candy.

Yes, everyone
was scared of big,
mean Bertha.
But no one was
more scared
than Max.

Max spent a lot of his time trying to avoid Big Bertha. He took the long way to school . . .

and the long way home.

And he never, ever walked down Dandelion Lane. That's where Bertha lived.

But no matter where Max went,
it seemed that Bertha was always
just one step behind him.

"I'm going to get you," Bertha called out from behind the old oak tree.

"I'm going to get you," she called out from behind Max's own father's car.

And poor Max was sure
that one day she would.

CHAPTER TWO:
Bully Busters

"You must learn to take care of yourself," Max's dad told him.

Then he signed up Max for karate class.

Max had lots of fun in karate class. He learned how to kick. He learned how to chop.

But the next time he saw Big Bertha, Max did exactly what he always did.

He ran the other way!

"You have to stand up for yourself," said Max's brother, Fred. "Just tell Bertha to leave you alone."

But Max did not think that was a very good idea.

"I bet Bertha would leave me alone if I had a dog," Max told his mother. "A big dog!"

But Max's sister, Lila, was afraid
of dogs—especially big ones. So
the dog they finally got was not
quite what Max had in mind.

Max named his new
dog Fang, but he knew
he wasn't fooling
anyone.

CHAPTER THREE:
Uh-oh, Here She Comes!

Max walked Fang every day.
Sometimes he walked Fang around
the block. Sometimes he walked
him to the park. And sometimes he
walked him all the way to Main
Street and back.

But he never, ever walked
him down Dandelion Lane.
In case you've forgotten ...
that's where Bertha lived.

One afternoon, Max took Fang to the playground. A bunch of kids were playing baseball there. They all gathered around to see Max's new dog.

"What a cute pup!" said Becky M.

"Isn't he sweet?" said Carole Anne, bending down to scratch Fang's ear.

"What kind of dog is he?" Paul asked.

"He's part Airedale," Max said proudly. "He—"

"He looks more like an air*head* to me," someone broke in.

Max's heart skipped a beat as he recognized the big, mean voice. Slowly, he turned around. And there, right behind him … was big, mean Bertha!

Uh-oh, thought Max. Now I'm going to get it.

But Bertha was already looking past him. "Give me that ball," she said to Paul.

Paul gave Bertha the ball.

Max wanted to tell Bertha to leave Paul alone. But when he opened his mouth, not a single word came out.

"Give me that airhead dog,"
Bertha suddenly said to Max.
"I want to see if he's smart
enough to catch the ball."

Max wanted to give Bertha
a high-flying karate kick. But
somehow he knew he couldn't
do it.

Bertha took a giant step toward
Max and grabbed Fang's leash.
"I guess you didn't hear me,"
she said in her biggest, meanest
voice. "GIVE ME THAT DOG!"

CHAPTER FOUR:
Back Off, Bertha!

More than anything, Max wanted to take a giant step back. But he couldn't do that, either. He couldn't leave Fang in Big Bertha's clutches.

There was a long moment of silence. Finally, Max took a deep breath. He yanked Fang's leash out of Bertha's hand and said, "NO!"

Then he took a giant step back.

Bertha could hardly believe her ears. The little kid was actually standing up to her.

Bertha stood there for a moment while she tried to figure out what to do next. At last, she turned to Becky M.

"Give me that mitt," she said.

Becky M. started to give Bertha the mitt. But then she looked at Max. He was still standing there, tightly clutching Fang's leash.

Becky M. snatched back her mitt. If Max could stand up to Bertha, so could she.

Bertha turned to Carole Anne.
Carole Anne was busy tapping dirt
off her shoe with the bat.

"Give me that bat," Bertha said.

Carole Anne just looked at
Bertha. She didn't even stop
tapping.

Bertha looked around at all the
kids. They were all looking back
at her. No one said a word. No one
moved an inch.

Bertha was the first to look away.
She looked down at the ground, and
there was Fang. He looked
up at her and wagged his tail.
   "*Woof*," Fang said just before
he licked Bertha's hand.

"Airhead," Bertha muttered
under her breath.
    And with that, she turned around
and stomped off down the street.

From that day on, Max was
no longer scared of Big Bertha.
Neither were his friends. As it
turned out, once everyone stopped
being so scared of Big Bertha,
she stopped being so scary.

And by the end of the year, she
didn't really seem so big, either!